THE STRANGE CASE OF
DR. JEKYLL
AND MR. HYDE

ROBERT LOUIS STEVENSON

CONDENSED AND ADAPTED BY
STEVE ROBINSON

ILLUSTRATED BY
JUERGEN WILLBARTH

Dalmatian 🐾 Press

The Dalmatian Press Children's Classics Collection
has been adapted and illustrated with care and thought,
to introduce you to a world of famous authors, characters, ideas,
and great stories that have been loved for generations.

Editor — Kathryn Knight
Creative Director — Gina Rhodes
And the entire classics project team of Dalmatian Press

ALL ART AND ADAPTED TEXT © DALMATIAN PRESS, LLC

ISBN: 1-57759-539-4 mass
1-57759-552-1 base

First Published in the United States in 2001 by Dalmatian Press, LLC, USA

Copyright © 2001 Dalmatian Press, LLC

Printed and bound in the U.S.A.

The DALMATIAN PRESS name and logo are
trademarks of Dalmatian Press, LLC, Franklin, Tennessee 37067.

11432

03 04 05 06 07 LBM 15 14 13 12 11 10 9 8 7 6

FOREWORD

A note to the reader—

A classic story rests in your hands. The characters are famous. The tale is timeless.

This Dalmatian Press Children's Classic has been carefully condensed and adapted from the original version (which you really *must* read when you're ready for every detail). We kept the well-known phrases for you. We kept the author's style. And we kept the important imagery and heart of each tale.

Literature is terrific fun! It encourages you to think. It helps you dream. It is full of heroes and villains, suspense and humor, adventure and wonder, and new ideas. It introduces you to writers who reach out across time to say: "Do you want to hear a story I wrote?"

Curl up and enjoy.

DALMATIAN PRESS
ILLUSTRATED CLASSICS

CONTENTS

CHARACTERS

MR. G.J. UTTERSON — a respected lawyer in London, an old friend to Dr. Lanyon and Dr. Jekyll

MR. RICHARD ENFIELD — Mr. Utterson's cousin, who points out "the door"

MR. EDWARD HYDE — a mysterious, deformed man with an evil personality

DR. HENRY JEKYLL — a respected, gentle doctor in London, who is haunted by secrets

DR. HASTIE LANYON — a friend to Utterson and Jekyll, whose jolly nature receives a shock

CHARACTERS

MR. POOLE — Dr. Jekyll's butler who is very worried about him

MR. BRADSHAW — a footman for Dr. Jekyll

MR. GUEST — Mr. Utterson's head law clerk, who can analyze handwriting

SIR DANVERS CAREW — a stately old gentleman who is murdered by Hyde

INSPECTOR NEWCOMEN — the chief detective for the Carew murder case

THE STRANGE CASE OF

DR. JEKYLL AND MR. HYDE

CHAPTER ONE

The Story of the Door

Mr. Utterson was a tall, handsome lawyer from London. He was rather quiet and he did not smile often. This made most people think he was a cold, dreary person. It *is* true that he was not comfortable talking with others. Yet there was something likable about him, though he kept very few close friends.

Utterson *did* enjoy having dinner with his friends from time to time. Some might call him snobbish, but he could, in fact, be kind and giving. He often helped those who had... let us say... gone down the wrong road. He noted to himself how some men had the "Devil" in them.

But he did not judge them. He used to say: "Every man has a secret and it's nobody's business but his own."

His good nature and few words made him welcome anywhere he went. He was very thankful for the good friends he had. His closest friends were those he had known the longest. No matter what trouble they were in, Utterson was a friend for life.

Mr. Richard Enfield was a distant cousin. He was a man-about-town in London who enjoyed Utterson's company. Their friendship seemed strange to some people because they didn't have much in common. They would take long Sunday walks, saying nothing and looking bored. Yet these walks were the highlight of their week. They turned down any offers from friends to do other things on Sundays—just so they could enjoy the day together.

On one of their Sunday walks, they ended up on a side street in one of the busy sections of London. The street was not like the rest of the neighborhood. It was freshly painted and clean. Though it was quiet on Sunday, the cheery shops looked like rows of smiling saleswomen.

The walk soon turned gloomy as the two men stopped in front of a sinister building that looked out of place. The walls were discolored and unpainted. The front had no windows. It had nothing but an ugly, evil-looking door with no bell or knocker. It was neglected and creepy.

Mr. Enfield lifted his cane and pointed it at the door. "Did you ever notice that door? I have an odd story to tell about it."

"Indeed," said Utterson flatly.

"Well, it was this way. I was walking home one night at three o'clock from… a nightspot. I found myself on a quiet, dark street lit with lamps. No one was out. I felt a sudden fear. I remember wishing there were a policeman nearby. All at once I saw two figures. A little man was stumbling quickly up one street. A girl of maybe five or six was running as fast as she could up the side street. The two ran into each other at the corner—and the man trampled calmly over the child's body. He left her screaming on the ground! It was a terrible thing to see. The man had an odd and disturbing look about him. I screamed for help as I grabbed the man around the neck.

"A crowd soon rushed over to comfort the child as I dragged the man back. He did not resist. He was so cool. The look he gave me made me feel sick and I began to sweat with fear. The child's family gathered and a doctor soon arrived. The child was not hurt badly, but was very scared.

"We all looked at this little man with disgust, as you might guess. The doctor was quite calm, but even *he* had a look of horror on his face. I thought the good doctor might kill him! Like the rest of us, he stared at the little man with rage. The doctor

looked at me and knew I had the same thoughts—but, of course, killing was not an answer. Instead, we threatened this wicked man and told him we would tell everyone we knew what had happened. The whole city of London would know about it—including any friends he had. I never saw such hateful faces. It was all we could do to keep the women from tearing him limb from limb.

"This twisted man had a dark, sneering face that made me think of a devil. This devil finally spoke and said, 'If you choose to make a big deal of this, then I am helpless. Name your price!'

"This took us by surprise. We quickly decided that the child's family should receive a good amount money—one hundred pounds. We followed the man to a place where he said he could pay us. Where do you think we found ourselves? Right here—at this ugly, evil door! He whipped out a key, went inside, and returned quickly with ten pounds in gold and a check for the rest. The check was signed by a man whose name I can't mention. It is a well-known name—often in the papers—and it is the reason I even tell this story. If the signature was *real*, then the check would definitely be good.

"The whole thing was very strange. I said to this devilish, dark villain that a man does not walk through a cellar door at four o'clock in the morning and return with another man's check. He sneered at me and offered to stay with us until the bank opened for business. We spent the next five hours at my home. After breakfast, we walked to the bank. I presented the check to the teller and said that I was sure it was a fake. Without delay I was told that it was genuine!"

"Oh, my," said Utterson.

"Yes. It's a bad story," continued Enfield. "This man I speak of was grotesque—simply awful. And the man who *signed* the check is a good, honest man—a fellow you know, in fact! Blackmail, I said to myself. This poor person who had signed the check must owe something to this little ugly man. Blackmail House is what I call this place with the door!"

"Does the man who signed the check live here?" asked Utterson with some interest.

"Good point. I happened to notice the address on the check. It was *not* this place with the door."

"Didn't you ever ask about the place with the door?" said Mr. Utterson.

"No, sir. I believe in leaving well enough alone. The stranger things look, the less I ask! But I have studied the place for myself. There is no other door. Rarely does anyone go in or out of it. There are only three windows on the other side and they're always shut. There is usually smoke coming from the chimney, so someone must live there."

The two walked in silence for a while, and then Utterson said, "I think you are right to leave well enough alone. A good rule to follow."

"Yes, I think it is," said Enfield.

"Still, there is one thing I'd like to know," said the lawyer. "What is the name of the man who walked over the child?"

"His name is Hyde. He is not easy to describe. There was something wrong with his face and body—something weird. I never saw a man I disliked more, but I can't really explain why. He was unusual. He was... well... deformed is the word I think of. I can picture him, but I can't describe him."

"Are you sure he had a key?" asked Utterson, after deep thought.

"My dear sir..." started Enfield, surprised.

"I'm sorry," said Utterson. "I know my question must seem strange. If I don't ask you the name of the man who signed the check, it is because I already know it. You see, Richard, your story hits home with me. If you left out anything, you better tell me now."

"I think you should have warned me that you knew about this place—before I went on and on," said Enfield. "I promise you that my story is true. This man had a key and still has it! I saw him use it one week ago!"

Mr. Utterson sighed deeply and said nothing.

"I should have kept my mouth shut. Let's never speak of this again," said Enfield.

"I will shake hands on that, Richard," said Utterson.

The two shook hands, then continued their walk in silence.

CHAPTER TWO

Dr. Jekyll's Will

That evening, Mr. Utterson came home to his bachelor house. He felt a little nervous as he sat down to dinner. Usually after dinner he would relax by the fire. But tonight he did not. He lit a candle, went into his office, and opened his safe. He removed an envelope that was marked:

Dr. Henry Jekyll's Will

He sat down at his desk and began to read the Will by candlelight. Mr. Utterson had not written the Will. It had been given to him to keep in secrecy. It said that if Dr. Henry Jekyll dies or turns out to be missing for three months, all of his money, his home, and everything in it should be passed on to his friend—*Edward Hyde*. This Will had always bothered Utterson. Reading it again didn't help. It bothered him that he did not know this Mr. Hyde. And now he knew that this man was a fiend—a cruel, heartless villain. Utterson felt confused and uncomfortable.

"I thought it was just madness that made Jekyll write this Will," he said out loud. "Now I know it was out of disgrace." He placed the Will back in the safe. Angrily, he grabbed his overcoat, blew out the dripping red candle, and walked out into the cool night. He needed to see his friend, Dr. Lanyon. If anyone could help him make sense of this, it was Lanyon.

The butler at the Lanyon home welcomed him and led him into the dining room. There, Dr. Lanyon sat alone sipping a glass of red wine. Lanyon was a dapper, red-faced gentleman with snow white hair and a loud, jolly voice. He rose from his chair as Utterson came in, and Lanyon shook his hand excitedly. The two had been friends since school days and had great respect for each other. They enjoyed each other's company.

After a little small talk, Utterson said, "Lanyon, you and I are probably Henry Jekyll's oldest friends. Would you agree?"

"I suppose we are," his friend replied, "but I see him very seldom these days."

"Really? I thought the two of you were close," said Utterson.

"We were. But about ten years ago, Jekyll became too odd for me. He began to go wrong— wrong in the mind. I think of him often, but have little desire to see him. We disagreed over some of his science theories. He spoke nonsense. His ideas were balderdash!" Lanyon turned purple. "Why do you ask?"

Utterson paused and then asked, "Have you ever met a certain friend of his—a Mr. Hyde?"

"Hyde?" asked Lanyon. "No. Never heard of him."

CHAPTER THREE

The Search for Hyde

Utterson returned home, learning nothing from Lanyon. In his large, dark bed, he tossed and turned as the night crept slowly by. Unanswered questions and fearful thoughts filled his mind.

The bells of the nearby church struck six o'clock as Utterson continued his sleepless night. He felt trapped as he tossed in the darkness of his room. Mr. Enfield's story went by in his mind like pictures in a book. He replayed the scene over and over: the little man, the screaming child, the family, the doctor, and finally the awful face of Hyde. But he saw no face really, only a blank figure in a nightmare with frantic people and a child who had been scared to death. He kept turning that story over in his mind—played out just like Enfield had explained it. He must meet this monster—this man mentioned in Dr. Jekyll's Will. He was sure that if he *did* meet him, he would hate him.

From that night on, Utterson made it his mission to find Mr. Hyde. He began to hang around the area of "the door." He was there in the mornings, again in the afternoon, and then he watched the door patiently by the light of the moon.

If he is Mr. Hyde, he thought, *I will be Mr. Seek.*

At last his patience was rewarded. It was a cold, dry night and the street lamps shone dimly through the fog. By ten o'clock, all the shops had closed and London was silent. Mr. Utterson stood at the corner near the mysterious door, watching and listening. Suddenly, he became aware of footsteps coming toward him. The steps grew louder as they came closer. Utterson eased his head from around the corner of the building and saw a small, plainly dressed man. The man quickly crossed the street and held out a key toward the door.

Utterson stepped out of the shadows and tapped the man on the shoulder as he passed.

"Mr. Hyde, I think?"

Mr. Hyde shrank back, hissing loudly, and would not look Utterson in the face. "That is my name. What do you want?"

"I see you are going in," said Utterson. "I am an old friend of Dr. Jekyll's. I am Utterson of Gaunt Street. Surely he has mentioned my name. I wonder if I could see him. I assume you are also

a friend, as I see you have a key to his home."

"I'm afraid Dr. Jekyll is not at home, Mr. Utterson," Hyde said, shielding his face. "How did you know me?"

"Ah, I could be wrong," said Utterson. "So, will you do me a favor?"

"With pleasure," replied Hyde. "What shall it be?"

"Will you let me see your face?"

Hyde hesitated. Then, with an air of cockiness, he jerked his head around and faced Utterson with a snarl. The two stared at each other.

"Now I will know you if I see you again. It's good to put a face with a name. It may be useful."

"Yes," said Mr. Hyde. "And it may be that you will need my address someday. I live in Soho—339 Blanchard Street."

He must know that I hold Jekyll's Will, thought Utterson.

"And now, Mr. Utterson," said Hyde, "how did you know me?"

"Just from conversations with friends we have in common," Utterson said.

"Friends in common?" Hyde said hoarsely. "Who are they?"

"Jekyll, for instance," said the lawyer.

Hyde's face became red. He leaned toward Utterson. "Why do you lie?" he cried.

"Such rude language," Utterson began.

With that, Hyde broke into a savage laugh. He quickly unlocked the door and disappeared into the house.

Utterson stood for a while in silence. Then he began to walk slowly up the street with his hand to his forehead. He was no less confused now than he was before the meeting. Mr. Hyde was pale and dwarfish, but not quite deformed. He had a displeasing smile. He acted both timid and bold, and spoke in a husky, whispering, broken voice. These qualities—all put together—disgusted and frightened Utterson. "The man seems hardly human," muttered Utterson. "He seems to have a beastly soul. O my poor friend Henry Jekyll. Are you truly a friend of this fiend who looks like a devil?"

Just around the corner from the cross street was a section of handsome houses. Utterson walked toward one of them and knocked loudly on the door. A well dressed, elderly servant opened the door.

"Is Dr. Jekyll at home, Poole?" asked the lawyer.

"I will see, Mr. Utterson," said the servant. He led the visitor into a large, low-roofed hall paved with flagstones. "Please wait here by the fire."

Utterson sat in a large leather chair. This familiar room had always been a comfortable place to Utterson. But tonight he shuddered as he looked into the fire. It brought back to his mind the evil face of Hyde, and he began to feel quite ill. He was somewhat relieved when Poole returned to say that Dr. Jekyll was out for the evening.

"I saw Mr. Hyde go in by the back door, Poole. Is that common when Dr. Jekyll is away?"

"Yes, sir," replied Poole. "Mr. Hyde has a key."

"Dr. Jekyll seems to have a great deal of trust in Mr. Hyde, Poole."

"Yes, sir, he does indeed," replied Poole. "We all have orders to obey him. We see very little of him, however. He never dines here. He mostly comes and goes through the laboratory door on the back side of the house."

"Well, give my best to Jekyll. Good night, Poole," said Utterson.

"I will, Mr. Utterson. Good night, sir."

The lawyer left the house of his friend with a heavy heart. He felt that Henry Jekyll was in deep trouble. Henry must have dark secrets. Indeed, Hyde was one of them. Was it possible that the ugly, evil man would do something dreadful to Jekyll? After all, he was named in Jekyll's Will as the only heir.

Night was falling and Utterson walked home in fear of something terrible yet to come.

CHAPTER FOUR

Dr. Jekyll's Promise

Two weeks later, it happened that Dr. Jekyll had a dinner party. He invited six of his closest friends, Dr. Utterson among them. After a fine meal and good conversation, the guests departed—all but Utterson. The lawyer sat down next to the roaring fire with his friend Henry Jekyll, to share his thoughts and concerns.

"I've been wanting to talk to you about your Will, Jekyll," started Utterson.

"My poor Utterson," said Jekyll, "I'm so sorry you have me for a client. I can see that you are very troubled. Has Lanyon been talking to you? He's a wonderful man, but, as you know, we are not speaking to each other."

Utterson wouldn't let Jekyll change the subject. "You know I never approved of the Will."

"My Will? Yes, I'm aware of that," said the doctor sharply. "You have told me that before."

"Well, I tell you again," continued the lawyer. "And I've learned a little about this Hyde character."

Jekyll's face turned white and his eyes darkened. "Don't say another word, Utterson. I thought we agreed not to discuss the Will again."

"What I've learned about Hyde disgusts me," said Utterson.

"I can't change that, my friend. You do not understand my position. I am in a peculiar, almost painful situation that I can do nothing about. Discussing it will not help or change a thing."

"Jekyll," said Utterson, "you know me. And I hope you trust me. Tell me what this young man has over you. Why in Heaven's name is he included in your Will? I can get you out of this mess."

"Utterson," said the doctor, "you are a good man—and a good friend. I will never find the

words to thank you for all you've done for me." Jekyll looked up at Utterson with sincere eyes. "To put your mind at ease, I will tell you this: whenever I want, I can be rid of Mr. Hyde. I give you my word on that. But this is a private matter. I ask you again to please forget about it."

Utterson stared into the fire. "I have no reason to doubt you," he said at last, standing slowly.

"Since we're on the subject of Hyde, I need to make one last point. I have a great interest in the poor man. I know you have seen him, for he told me so. I fear he was rude. But he is of great concern to me. If I am taken away, Utterson, you must promise me that you will deal fairly with him and give him what I state in my Will. If I could tell you everything, I have no doubt that you would agree with me."

"I can't pretend that I'll ever like him," said the lawyer.

"And I don't ask you to," pleaded Jekyll, laying his hand on his friend's shoulder. "I only ask that you help him for my sake when I am no longer here."

Utterson sighed deeply. "I promise."

CHAPTER FIVE

The Murder

Nearly a year later, in October, the people of London were startled by a terrible crime. It was witnessed by a maidservant who lived alone in a house not far from the river.

The maid had gone upstairs to bed around 11:00 P.M. She was in a dreamy mood, and for a while she sat in her favorite wicker chair staring out her window. The fog was beginning to settle in, but the lane below was still lit by the full moon. It was a lovely night, she remembered. But not for long.

She noticed a handsome elderly gentleman with white hair. He was strolling down the lane.

In the moonlight she could see his kind face and gentle expression. Coming toward him was a small gentleman dressed in black. She did not take much notice of the small man—until the two men met right below her window.

The older man bowed and spoke in a polite manner. He seemed to be asking directions from the small man. The maid was not trying to hear the words. She was more interested in the old man's face. It shone in the moonlight and his expression was calm—beautiful, in fact. He had that old-world charm, being at peace with himself and the world.

Then her eye wandered to the other man. She was surprised to recognize him as Mr. Hyde. She knew him because he once visited her master at the home where she worked most weekdays. She had immediately disliked him that day. And now she studied him as he stood below her window. Hyde was carrying a heavy wooden cane. He kept fidgeting with it as if he were nervous. He didn't answer the kind old man's words. Instead, this small man appeared impatient and never looked the old gentleman in the eye.

All of a sudden, Hyde began to stomp his feet. He waved his cane in the air like a madman. The older gentleman took a step back in surprise and confusion. Then Hyde's cane came down on the man—again and again. The bewildered gentleman fell to his knees and crumpled upon the street. Hyde continued to hit the man with his cane and trample upon his lifeless body. An enraged, evil soul was stamping out the goodness it saw in a kind old man. The horror was too much for the maid, and she fainted.

CHAPTER SIX

The Hunt for Hyde

It was two o'clock in the morning when the maid finally woke up and sent for the police. The murderer was long gone. But there, in the middle of the lane, lay the body of the old gentleman.

The police arrived and searched the area. Lying near the body was one half of the finely-made wooden cane, bloody and broken. They found a change purse and gold watch on the body, but no papers except for one envelope. The envelope was sealed and stamped. The gentleman had probably been carrying it to the post office. It was addressed to Mr. G.J. Utterson.

A policeman took the envelope to Utterson early the next morning. The lawyer was briefly told of the murder.

"I will say nothing until I see the body," Utterson said with a serious face.

At the police station, Utterson entered the cell and nodded. "I am sorry to say that this is Sir Danvers Carew."

"Good heavens, sir," exclaimed the officer, "are you sure? This will make a great deal of noise in the town. Carew was a fine man—well liked and respected."

"I'm afraid you are right," said Utterson sadly.

"Perhaps you can help us," said the officer. He retold the maid's story of seeing Hyde and showed Utterson the broken cane.

Utterson felt ill at the sound of Hyde's name. When he saw the cane, he had no doubt that Hyde was the murderer. Even though the top part of the cane was missing, he knew it was the cane he himself had given to his friend, Dr. Henry Jekyll, many years before.

"Is this Mr. Hyde a small man?" asked Utterson.

"The maid described him as small and wicked looking," said the officer.

Utterson thought for a moment, then said, "If you will join me in my cab, I think I can take you to his house in Soho."

At 9:00 they arrived in Soho, a dismal section of town, covered in morning fog. They found 339 Blanchard, the address Hyde had given Utterson. Ragged women and children huddled in the doorways. The street was filthy. Utterson could not believe how awful Soho looked. *This is the home of the favorite friend of Dr. Henry Jekyll?* he thought. *A man who would inherit Jekyll's fortune?*

A pale, silver-haired woman opened the door. Yes, she told them, Hyde lived here, but he was not at home. He had been in that night very late, but he had gone away again within an hour. She explained that he came and went at odd times, and that he was often absent. For instance, last night was the first she had seen of him in nearly two months.

"Well then, we'd like to see his rooms," said the lawyer. The woman looked away and began to close the door, but Utterson continued, "This is Inspector Newcomen of Scotland Yard."

"Ah!" she said with a wicked smile. "He's in trouble, isn't he?"

She led them through the empty house to the rooms where Hyde stayed. They were decorated and furnished very nicely. However, the place looked as if it had been ransacked. Clothes were pulled out of drawers. The fireplace held new ashes, as if papers had been burned. Sticking out of the ashes, half burned, was a green checkbook. Behind the door the officer found the other half of the cane.

The inspector was delighted. Never had he recovered so much evidence so quickly.

As it turned out, however, Hyde was not easy to find. There were no records of him. No family could be found. He had never been photographed. Few people had ever seen him, and they gave different descriptions of him. Anyone who had ever met Hyde did agree on one thing—there was something deformed and evil about him.

CHAPTER SEVEN

The Letter

It was late in the afternoon when Mr. Utterson arrived at Dr. Jekyll's door. Poole led him through the house to the kitchen, then out and across a yard which had once been a garden. At the back of the yard was the large building which was known as the laboratory. The doctor had bought this building from the children of a famous surgeon, and he had turned it into a laboratory. Utterson knew the front of this very building. It was the building with "the door" on the front side that faced the street. There were not many people, besides Utterson, who knew that Jekyll owned this building. In fact, it was the first time that Utterson had actually been inside the laboratory, and he felt uneasy.

The tables were covered with chemical bottles and equipment for science experiments. On the floor was a messy heap of crates and packing straw. The windows were dirty and dark. At the far end of the room, a flight of stairs led to a door which Utterson now entered. Utterson stepped into Jekyll's office, a large room with very little light. Close to the fireplace was a large antique desk. There sat Jekyll, looking deathly ill. The doctor dismissed Poole, but did not stand to greet Utterson. He just held out a cold hand and asked, in a hoarse voice, for him to sit down.

"Dr. Jekyll," said Utterson, "I assume you have heard the news of the murder."

The doctor shuddered. "They have been crying it in the streets all day."

"I must ask you one thing," said the lawyer. "Danvers Carew was my client. You are also my client. I don't know which to serve. I know that Hyde is your… friend. Please tell me that you are not crazy enough to hide this murderer."

"Utterson, I swear," cried the doctor, "I swear to Heaven, I will never set eyes on him again.

I give you my word of honor that I am done with him. It is all at an end. And indeed, he does not want my help. You do not know him as I do. He is safe, he is quite safe. Mark my words, he will never be heard from again."

Utterson listened gloomily, thinking his friend looked very ill. "You seem sure of him," he said, "and for your sake, I hope you are right. If it came to a trial, your name would surely come up."

"I am quite sure of him," replied Jekyll. "I am absolutely certain, but I cannot tell you why. There is one thing that you can help me with—as my lawyer. I have… I have received a letter. I don't know if I should show it to the police. I'll give it to you and trust that you'll do what's best with it."

"Do you think this letter may lead to Hyde's arrest?" asked the lawyer.

"No," said Jekyll. "I don't care what becomes of Hyde. I am quite done with him. I am concerned, however, about my own reputation."

"Let me see the letter," said Utterson.

The letter was written in an odd, left-slanting handwriting and signed "Edward Hyde." It said that Dr. Jekyll should not worry about the writer's safety. He had a way to escape and was thankful for all Jekyll had done for him in the past.

"Where is the envelope?" asked Utterson.

"I burned it," replied Jekyll, "before I knew what it was about. But it had no postmark. The note was hand-delivered."

"Shall I keep it and look it over more closely?" asked Utterson.

"Yes," replied Jekyll, "I have complete trust in you. I have lost trust in myself."

"One more question," said the lawyer. "Was it Hyde who told you how to word your Will—that he should receive everything if you should disappear?"

The doctor covered his face with his hands and nodded, saying, "O God, Utterson, what a mistake I have made and what a lesson I have learned."

"I knew it," said Utterson. "I think he meant to murder you."

On his way out of the main house, the lawyer had a word with Poole. "There was a letter delivered by hand today. What was the messenger like?" But Poole was positive nothing had come but regular post mail.

This news sent Utterson home with more fears. The letter must have come through the street-side door of the laboratory. Or, possibly, it was written in Jekyll's own office. Utterson was afraid that this might be the case. Did he truly want to know the answer to this mystery if it brought shame to his friend's name?

CHAPTER EIGHT

The Comparison

Utterson sat in his own office with a warm fire in the hearth. His head clerk, Mr. Guest, was with him, enjoying small talk. *This is a man I trust*, thought Utterson, looking at Guest. Even lawyers need advice, and Utterson needed advice on what to do with Hyde's note to Jekyll. Guest was a man who studied handwriting. Perhaps Hyde's handwriting would tell them more about the strange man. Mr. Guest had been to Jekyll's home several times and knew Poole. In addition, Mr. Guest could keep a secret. Utterson decided to bring the matter up.

"It's sad about Sir Danvers," the lawyer said.

"Yes, sir, it is indeed," said the clerk. "Everyone is talking about it. The murderer must have been insane!"

"I'd like to hear your views on that," replied Utterson. "I have a note here written and signed by the murderer."

Guest's eyes brightened.

Utterson quickly said, "But, Guest, no one can know that you've seen it."

Mr. Guest sat down at the desk at once to study the letter.

"Well, sir, it is not the handwriting of someone who is insane. It *is* odd-looking, though," the clerk said at last, deep in thought.

"Well, it *is* from a very odd writer," Utterson said.

Just then, a servant entered the room with a note. Utterson remarked that it was an invitation to dinner—from Dr. Jekyll.

"Ah! From Dr. Jekyll?" asked Mr. Guest with great interest.

"It is indeed," said the lawyer. "Would you like to see it?"

"If I may, sir. Thank you, sir." The clerk laid the two notes side by side on the desk. He studied first one, then the other. "Thank you, sir," he said, handing the notes back to Utterson. "Very interesting. Very interesting, indeed."

"Why did you compare them?" asked Utterson with concern showing on his face.

"Well, sir," replied the clerk, "the writing on the two notes is very much alike. Almost the same, in fact. However, one handwriting slants to the left, and the other slants to the right. That's really the only difference."

"Interesting," said the lawyer.

"Rather interesting," added Guest.

"This is to be kept between us, Guest."

"Yes, sir. I understand," said Guest with a casual bow.

Mr. Utterson locked the invitation from Jekyll and the note in his safe. He was shaken by what Mr. Guest had said. *What!* he thought. *Would Henry Jekyll write and sign a note—and say it was from Hyde? Why would Jekyll forge for a murderer?* Utterson became cold with fear.

CHAPTER NINE

A Visit with Dr. Lanyon

Time passed with no sign of Mr. Hyde. He had disappeared as if he had never existed. A great deal of money was offered in reward for any information leading to his arrest. Many people came forward with stories of this horrible man. He was described as deformed, cruel, evil, and violent. He was said to be friends with strange people. But no one knew where he was. He had simply vanished.

After a while, Mr. Utterson began to recover from the nightmares that had kept him up every night. Sir Danvers was gone, but so was Hyde— and that was one good thing from all this.

Now that the evil Mr. Hyde was gone, Jekyll seemed to be his old self again. He came out more, saw friends, and was once again a lively guest. He found ways to help those in need, and he went to church more often. He stayed very busy, and his face looked happier and brighter. For more than two months, the doctor was at peace.

On the 8th of January, Utterson dined at the doctor's house with several good friends. Even Dr. Lanyon was there. It was just like the old days. Utterson, Jekyll, and Lanyon were the close trio of friends they had once been.

Utterson saw Jekyll almost every day after that. But then, on the 12th, and again on the 14th, Poole told Utterson that Jekyll would see no one. On the 15th, Poole said that the doctor had locked himself in his room. The lawyer visited the next five days, but got the same answer. Utterson became upset by this sudden change. Finally, one night he went to dine with Dr. Lanyon.

Utterson was looking forward to seeing Lanyon. When he arrived, however, he was shocked by how Lanyon had changed. He had the look of death on his face. The rosy man had

become pale and thin, as if he had aged ten years. But something bothered Utterson even more. It was the look in Lanyon's eye—a look of terror.

"My dear friend," said Utterson carefully, "you look very ill."

"I have had a terrible shock," answered the doctor, "and I shall never recover. If I last a month, I'll be surprised. Life has been good. I liked it. At least, I used to like it, my friend. I think it is better that we don't know all there is to know in this world…"

"Jekyll is sick, too," said Utterson. "Have you seen him?"

But Lanyon's face changed, and he held up his trembling hand. "As far as I'm concerned, Jekyll is dead," he said in a loud, unsteady voice. It was a voice Utterson had never heard from his friend. "I have no desire to ever see or speak to him again."

"What you're saying bothers me terribly, my friend," said Utterson. "The three of us have been friends for so long. At our age, it will be difficult to form another friendship as strong as ours."

"Nothing can be done," answered Lanyon. "Ask him yourself."

"He refuses to see me," said the lawyer.

"I'm not surprised to hear that," Lanyon replied. "Some day, Utterson, after I am dead, you'll learn what this is all about. I cannot be the one to tell you. If you wish to sit and talk of other things, then stay. If you do not, then please go, for I cannot take another minute of this."

CHAPTER TEN

The Loss of Two Friends

As soon as he got home, Utterson wrote a letter to Jekyll. He complained about not being able to see him. He wrote about his visit with their sick friend, Lanyon. He also wrote what Lanyon had said about Jekyll.

The next day, Utterson received a letter in response. It was poorly written with sloppy lettering. This was odd because Jekyll was a very good writer. "There's nothing that can be done about Lanyon and me," it began. "I do not blame our old friend, and I agree with him that we should never meet again. From now on, my friend Utterson, I must keep my distance from all people. But please know that I will never doubt our friendship. You must let me go my own dark way. I am a sinner, and so I must suffer. I could not stand to have you see the pain I am in. I've brought it all upon myself. You must respect my wishes and leave me alone in silence."

Utterson was amazed and confused. Even though Hyde was gone, Jekyll had returned to this madness. A week before, he had been his old self, smiling and cheerful. First Lanyon's mysterious illness. Now Jekyll's demand to be alone. What were the deep, dark secrets hiding behind these matters?

Just one week later, Dr. Lanyon became bed-bound. Within two weeks he was dead. The night after the funeral, Utterson sat at his desk with one lone candle lit. Before him was an envelope with Dr. Lanyon's handwriting on the front. It read:

PRIVATE: for G.J. Utterson
Upon My Death
If Utterson should die before me,
then this letter is to be destroyed.

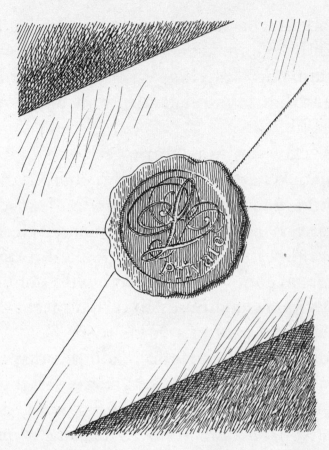

Utterson sighed deeply. *I have buried one friend today*, he thought. *What if this should cost me another?* He broke the seal and opened the envelope. Inside he found a smaller envelope which read:

Not To Be Opened
Until the Death or Disappearance
of Dr. Henry Jekyll

Utterson sat back in his chair. He could not believe it. Here were the same instructions that were on Jekyll's Will! But Jekyll had admitted that Hyde had told him what to write for the Will, so...

The lawyer was tempted to open the envelope. What would he find inside? But his own honor and his faith in his friend were more important than what might be inside. He placed the envelope into his safe and locked it tightly.

Utterson continued to visit Jekyll's home every few days. Poole continued to turn him away. Poole said that the doctor was in his room nearly all the time now. He had given up reading and speaking. Poole was not even sure Jekyll was sleeping—he just sat staring, as if he had lost his mind.

Utterson became used to hearing these sad reports about his friend. After awhile, he no longer stopped by to hear them.

CHAPTER ELEVEN

The Window

On Sunday, Mr. Utterson was on his usual walk with Mr. Enfield. They ambled along the quiet streets and came upon "the door." Both stopped and stared at it.

"Well," said Enfield, "*that* story is at an end at least. We shall never see more of Mr. Hyde."

"I hope not," said Utterson. "Did I ever tell you that I saw him once? He was an ugly man, just as you said."

"He was that and more," said Enfield. "And by the way, what a fool I was not to know that this was a back way into Jekyll's home."

"So you found it out, did you?" said Utterson.

"Well, if that's the case, let's step into the courtyard and take a look at the windows. To tell you the truth, I'm worried about poor Jekyll. Maybe we'll see him and be able to get his attention. That might do him some good."

The courtyard was cool and damp, dimly lit by the afternoon sun. One side window was open. Sitting inside, close to the window, was Dr. Jekyll. He looked like a sad prisoner.

"Jekyll!" cried Utterson. "Are you feeling better?"

"I am very low, Utterson," replied the doctor drearily, "very low. It will not last long, thank God."

"You stay indoors too much," said the lawyer. "You should be out with us. This is Mr. Enfield, my cousin. Why don't you join us for a brisk walk? It will certainly do you good!"

"I would like that very much," sighed the doctor, "but no, no, no, it is impossible. I dare not. I am glad to see you, though. I would ask you in, but this place is really not fit for guests."

"Well, then," said the lawyer, "we'll just talk to you from the courtyard."

"That's just what I was about to say,"

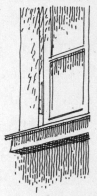

returned the doctor with a smile. Then, suddenly, the smile was gone from his face. His face twisted into a look of terror and despair. It froze the blood of Utterson and Enfield. The window was slammed shut without warning. The two men left the courtyard with horror in their eyes.

When they had walked back out to the street, Utterson turned to his cousin and muttered, "Heaven help us. Heaven help us."

But Mr. Enfield only nodded his head very seriously, and walked on in silence.

CHAPTER TWELVE

The Last Night

Utterson was sitting by his fire one evening after dinner when a visitor surprised him. It was Jekyll's butler, Poole.

"Bless me, Poole, what brings you here?" he cried. "Are you all right? Is something the matter with Dr. Jekyll?"

"Mr. Utterson," said Poole, "there is something wrong."

"Take a seat," said the lawyer. "I'll pour you something to drink. Now, take your time and tell me what you want."

"You know how the doctor has been, sir," said Poole. "You know how he has shut himself in.

Well, he's locked himself in his office above the laboratory. I'm so afraid…"

"My good man," Utterson said quietly, "what exactly is it that frightens you?"

Poole gazed into the fire, never once meeting Utterson's eyes. The glass rested on his knee, untouched. "I can't take it anymore!" he finally said, looking terrified.

"Try to calm down," said the lawyer, "and tell me what's wrong."

"I think here has been foul play," said Poole hoarsely.

"Foul play?" cried the lawyer. "What can you mean?"

"I think, sir," he answered, "that you should come with me and see for yourself."

Utterson grabbed his hat and coat and rushed out.

It was a cold March night with a pale moon high in the sky. The wind was strong and made talking difficult. The streets were bare. Utterson had never seen this part of London so deserted. He walked in silence, wondering what was wrong at Jekyll's home. Poole looked so white and frightened. They arrived at the house and Poole turned to Utterson with relief.

"Well, sir," he said in a broken voice, "here we are. God grant there be nothing wrong."

"Amen, Poole," said the lawyer.

Poole knocked. The door was opened, but it was chained. A voice from inside asked, "Is that you, Poole?"

"It's all right," said Poole. "Open the door."

The door opened slowly and they entered the main hallway. It was brightly lit with a raging fire in the fireplace. Dr. Jekyll's entire staff was there, huddled like a flock of sheep. At the sight

of Mr. Utterson, the housemaid began to weep. The cook cried out, "Thank God, it's Mr. Utterson," as she ran to take him in her arms.

"I can't believe you're all here," said the lawyer, "and not at your work stations."

"They're all afraid to be alone," said Poole.

Silence followed for several moments until the maid again began to weep loudly.

"Please control yourself," cried Poole.

They all turned toward the inner door with a look of fear on their faces. Poole took a candle from the hearth and asked Utterson to follow. They made their way out to the back garden very slowly.

"Please, sir," said Poole, "you must be silent. I want you to hear, and I don't want you to be heard. If he does by chance invite you in, don't go!"

Utterson felt his knees begin to shake. He followed Poole through the courtyard, into the laboratory, and to the steps that led to Jekyll's office. Poole walked up the steps gently, as if he were sneaking up on the door. He whispered to Utterson to come up and put his ear to the door. Then Poole knocked three times.

"Mr. Utterson would like to see you, sir," he called.

A voice answered from within. "Tell him I cannot see anyone," it said angrily.

"Thank you, sir," said Poole. He led Mr. Utterson back across the yard and into the huge kitchen where the fire was out and the beetles scurried on the floor.

"Sir," he said, looking Mr. Utterson in the eyes, "was that my master's voice?"

"It seems to have changed," replied the lawyer, who had grown pale.

"Changed? Well, yes, I'd say it has," said the butler. "I've worked for this man in this house for twenty years. I tell you, Utterson, that was not my master's voice! Eight days ago we heard him cry out to God. As of that time, someone else has taken his place! Dr. Jekyll is not in that room! Who is in there? And why does it stay there? This is something most evil, Mr. Utterson!"

"This is a very strange tale, Poole, a rather wild tale, my man," said Utterson, biting his finger. "What if—what if, as you fear, that the doctor has been—well, murdered. Why would the murderer stay in his office? This makes no sense, Poole!"

"Well, Mr. Utterson, let me explain some more. Maybe then you will believe me," said Poole. "All this week, that man—or thing—has been living in the office. Day and night he has been crying out for some kind of medicine. He leaves notes on the stairs outside the office asking for food and medicine. We leave the food

or drugs on the stair and he sneaks it in when we don't see. Sometimes three times a day I receive orders to buy medicine from drug stores in the London area. And every time he cries out that the drugs are no good. But the orders for these chemicals and drugs keep coming. Still, he cries all through the night."

"Do you have any of these written orders?" asked Mr. Utterson.

Poole reached into his pocket and handed the lawyer a crumpled piece paper. Utterson held it near the candle to see it more clearly. It was a short note written to a local drug store, thanking them for the good service and drugs they had mixed for Jekyll many years before. It went on to explain that lately he had been receiving the wrong mixture, which was dangerous. The letter ended: "For God's sake, mix the chemicals the way you used to—and send them immediately!" It was signed: "Dr. Jekyll."

"This is a strange note," said Utterson. "Is this Jekyll's handwriting?"

"I thought it looked like it," the servant said sadly, "but I saw the man and I doubt it."

"You saw him?" said Utterson. "When? I thought he'd been locked up all this time."

"I saw him!" said Poole. "I walked into the lab one night and he was looking through the crates. I guess he was looking for drugs. He looked up when I came in, and cried out in anger. He quickly ran up the stairs to the office. I only saw him for a second, but it made me shiver. Sir, if it was my master, why did he have a mask on his face? If it was my master, why did he cry like a rat and run from me? I have served him for so long!" Poole paused and covered his face with his trembling hands. He was obviously scared to death.

"This is all very odd, Poole, but I think I'm beginning to understand. Your master must have a rare disease—a disease which tortures and deforms him. Thus the mask and the need to avoid his friends; thus the eagerness to find this drug, which, in his mind, is his only hope. God help him! That's got to be the truth, Poole. If not, I am not sure that we want to know the truth."

"Sir," said the butler, "that thing was not my master, and there's the truth! My master," he whispered, "is a tall, well-built man, and this was more of a dwarf."

Utterson attempted to interrupt.

"Sir," cried Poole, "don't you think I know my master after twenty years? After all this time, don't I know how tall he is and how he walks and talks? No, sir, that thing in the mask was never Dr. Jekyll. God knows what it was, but it was never Dr. Jekyll! I believe in my heart, Mr. Utterson, that there has been a murder!"

"I trust you, Poole," replied the lawyer. "The details here are not clear. And I certainly do not want to hurt my friend Jekyll in any way. Still, I think that we have no option but to break down that door!"

"Ah, Mr. Utterson, now you're talking!" cried the butler. "We'll do it together. There's an axe in the laboratory, and here is a heavy iron kitchen poker. I'm scared, Mr. Utterson, but I'm also relieved."

The lawyer held the poker in his hand and said, "Poole, it's entirely possible that you and I are about to break this door down and see things no man should ever want to see."

"I have the same feelings, sir, but I know that we have to do it," returned the butler.

"Before we do this," said Utterson, "let me ask you something. This man… or thing that you saw… did you recognize it?"

"Well, sir, it happened so quickly, and the creature was hunched over. I could not swear to it, but if you are asking if it was Mr. Hyde, yes, I think it was! It was the same size and moved the same way. And who else had a key to the laboratory door? Don't forget, sir, that at the time of Carew's murder, Hyde still had the key with him. But that's not all. I don't know, Mr. Utterson, if you ever met this Mr. Hyde?"

"Yes," said the lawyer, "I once spoke with him."

"Then you must know as well as the rest of us that there was something sinister about that gentleman—something that made me weak. I don't know exactly how to say it, sir, except to say that he made me feel cold—right down to the bone!"

"That is just how I felt," said Mr. Utterson.

"Well, sir," replied Poole, "when that masked thing jumped like a monkey, knocked over the crates, and scurried into the office, a chill went down my spine like ice. Oh, I know that's not evidence, Mr. Utterson, but I give you my word, that man was Hyde!"

"Aye, aye," said the lawyer, "I fear the same thing. I believe there is evil in that room—evil we could never imagine. I believe poor Henry is dead. I believe the murderer is still lurking in his victim's room. We will have revenge, Poole. Call Bradshaw."

The footman came in quickly, very white and nervous.

"Try to stay calm, Bradshaw," said the lawyer. "This suspense has worn you all down. But it is time to end this madness. Poole and I are going to force our way into the office. If this turns out to be a mistake, I'll take the blame. However, if things *are* as they seem, you and the errand boy must be ready at the back entrance in case he tries to escape through the laboratory. Arm yourselves with clubs. We'll give you ten minutes to get to your posts."

CHAPTER THIRTEEN

The Discovery

As Bradshaw left, the lawyer looked at his watch. "And now, Poole, we must get to our *own* posts. It is time to gather every ounce of courage we own and know that we are doing the right thing," he said. Taking the iron poker under his arm, he led the way into the yard under a dark sky. They stepped into the laboratory and sat down silently to wait. The sound of pacing could be heard on the office's old floor above.

"That's the way it has been day and night, except when a new sample comes from the druggist. Then there's a bit of a break. And, Mr. Utterson, tell me, is that the doctor's walk?

Did he walk in slow, sliding steps? No, sir! He walked with a long, confident stride!"

The steps sounded light and off-balance. It was different indeed from the heavy creaking steps of Henry Jekyll. Utterson sighed. "Does he do anything else?"

Poole nodded. "Once," he said. "Once I heard it weeping. Like a woman or a lost soul. I came away almost in tears myself."

Ten minutes passed. Utterson picked up the poker with sweaty palms and walked toward the door. The candle was set on the table to light their attack. They drew near. Jekyll kept his constant pace, up and down, up and down, in the quiet of the night.

"Jekyll!" cried Utterson, with a loud voice. "I demand to see you!" He paused, but there was no answer. "I warn you! We are suspicious of what is beyond this door. If you do not open it this minute, we will break it down by force!"

"Utterson," said the voice, "for God's sake, have mercy!"

"Ah, that is not Jekyll's voice—it's Hyde's!" cried Utterson. "Break down the door, Poole!"

Poole swung the axe over his shoulder.

The blow shook the building. The door leaped against its lock and hinges. A dismal screech, like that of a wild animal, rang from the office. Up went the axe again, and again the panels crashed and splintered. Four times the axe came down and still the ancient door did not break. On the fifth, Poole gave it all he had. The lock burst and the door fell inward to the floor with a crash.

The two men, shocked by the noise, stood back a little and peered in. There lay the office in the quiet lamplight, a good fire glowing on the hearth. The doctor's desk was neatly stacked with paperwork. They heard a kettle whistling, and saw a table laid out for tea. It was a quiet room—a common room, except for the bottles of chemicals.

Right in the middle of the room there lay the body of a man, curled up and still twitching. They walked toward it with careful steps, turned it on its back, and looked into its face. It was Edward Hyde. He was dressed in clothes far too large for him. He had a small crushed glass vial in his right hand. There was a smell of poison in the air. Utterson knew that he was looking on a man who had just taken his own life.

"We've come too late," he said sternly.

"Whether we wanted to save or destroy him, Hyde is dead. Now, Poole, we must find the body of your master."

Utterson and Poole walked through the entire ground floor as well as the office, which overlooked the courtyard. A hallway led from the street door to the main laboratory and connected to another flight of stairs that led to the office. There were dark closets everywhere, and a large cellar. The closets were all empty and dusty, as if they had not been used in years. The cellar was filled with rotten lumber, dating back to the days the surgeon had owned the home. They searched every nook, but there was no trace of Henry Jekyll, dead or alive.

Poole stomped on the flagstones of the hallway. "He must be buried here," he said. "There's a hollow sound."

"Or he may have escaped to the alleyway through this door," said Utterson. He examined the door. It was locked. He kicked something metal and picked up a rusted key.

"Look, sir," said Poole, "this key is bent, as if someone had stomped on it."

"Aye," said Utterson, "and it's rusty. It has

been here a while."

The two men looked at each other. "This is beyond me, Poole," said the lawyer. "Let's go back to the office."

They climbed the stairs in silence. Looking now and then at the dead body, they began to search the office more carefully. At one table, there were bottles and traces of chemicals. A white salt-like powder was piled on a glass plate, as though for an experiment which the poor man never got to finish.

"That is the same drug that I was always bringing him," said Poole.

Their own reflections in a full length mirror startled them. "This mirror has seen some strange things, sir," whispered Poole. "Why would he have a mirror like this in his office?"

Utterson stared deeply into the mirror, in horror at the thought of stories it could tell. "I know what you're thinking, Poole," said Utterson.

Next they turned to the desk. Here they found family pictures and personal papers of Jekyll's that Hyde had obviously tried to destroy in his anger.

Among the papers they found a large envelope

addressed to Mr. Utterson. The lawyer opened it and several papers fell to the floor. The first was the Will that Jekyll had drawn up, leaving everything to Hyde. But in place of the name of Edward Hyde, the lawyer read with amazement the name of Gabriel John Utterson! He looked at Poole, then back at the paper, and lastly at the dead body stretched out on the carpet.

"My head goes round," said Utterson. "This man lying here could not possibly have liked me. Yet he must have seen this Will. I can't believe he didn't destroy it."

He looked at the next paper. It was a brief note written by the doctor and dated at the top.

"Oh, Poole!" cried the lawyer, "this is dated this very day! He was alive and here today! He could not have been killed and hidden in such a short time. He must still be alive! He must have escaped! But why? And how? And can we really say this is a suicide? I'm afraid there is more to this!"

"Why don't you read it, sir?" asked Poole.

"Because I'm afraid," replied Utterson. "I wish I didn't have to… but I have no choice, do I?" Taking a deep breath, he brought the paper closer and read:

My Dear Utterson,
When you receive this, I will have disappeared. As I write this, I know the end is near. First, you must read the letter you received from Lanyon. He warned me he had given it to you. Knowing you, it is in your safe at home and you have not yet read it. Then, if you want to know more, turn to the confession of:
Your unworthy and unhappy friend,
Henry Jekyll

"Confession? Is there a third paper?" asked Utterson.

"Here, sir," said Poole. He handed Utterson a sealed packet.

The lawyer put it in his pocket. "Don't tell anyone about these papers. If your master has escaped or is dead, maybe we can at least save his good name. It's ten o'clock. I'm going home to read these in quiet. I'll be back by midnight and then we'll send for the police."

They went out, locking the lab door behind them. Utterson walked quickly back to his office to read Lanyon's letter and Jekyll's confession. The mystery would finally be explained.

CHAPTER FOURTEEN

Dr. Lanyon's Letter

Utterson opened his safe and pulled out the letter from Lanyon. In the quiet of his office he read:

Dear Utterson,

Four days ago, on January 9th, I received a registered letter, sent by my old friend Henry Jekyll. This surprised me. We had never sent each other letters, and I had just had dinner with him the night before. I grew even more curious as I read the letter. It said:

Dear Lanyon,

You are one of my oldest friends. We have disagreed at times, but you have been a true friend, and I would do anything in the world for you. Lanyon, my life, my honor, and my sanity are all in your hands. If you fail me tonight, I will be lost forever. You may be thinking that I'm about to ask you to do something unlawful. Please keep reading and decide for yourself.

No matter what you may have planned for this evening, I'm begging you to cancel! Take a cab or your carriage and drive straight to my house. Poole, my butler, has orders to expect you and allow you into my home. I've also asked him to call for a locksmith. You are to force open the door of my laboratory office and go in alone. In my office you will find a cabinet marked with an "E" which may be locked. If it is, have the locksmith open it. Open the fourth drawer down from the top. There you should find some powders, a vial, and a paper book. Remove the drawer from the cabinet and take it back to your home on Cavendish Square.

If you leave immediately after reading this, you should be home before midnight.

At exactly midnight, please be in your office. You will hear a knock at the door from a man answering in my name. Give him the file cabinet drawer. I will be thankful to you more than you can know. Five minutes after you hand over the drawer, you will understand how important this is to me. If you cannot help me, I will go completely insane and will die the most horrible death.

I'm hoping that you will be able to do this for me, my friend. I am trembling in fear that you won't. I'm in a strange and dark place—in a blackness of distress you could never understand. If you can help me, all of my troubles will be gone. Help me, Lanyon! I beg you, please help me!

Your friend, Henry Jekyll

P.S. I just had a horrible thought. If the mail reaches you a day late, follow the instructions anyway on whatever day you read this. I will know if you have the drawer, and you can expect a midnight knock. If the night passes with no knock at your door, you will know that you have seen the last of Henry Jekyll.

After I read the letter, I knew that Jekyll must be insane. But until that was proven, I knew I must help him and follow his instructions. The less I knew the better. All I really needed to know was that my friend needed help. I got up from my desk, got into my carriage, and drove straight to Jekyll's house.

The butler was waiting at the door when I arrived. He, too, had received a registered letter with instructions. He had called for a locksmith and carpenter. The four of us walked through the home

and garden and then into the laboratory building. The door to Jekyll's office was very strong and the lock was excellent. The carpenter and locksmith spent almost two hours working, but, finally, the door swung open. The cabinet marked "E" was not locked. I removed the fourth drawer. I filled it with straw and wrapped it up in a cloth. Then I left, taking the entire drawer to my home.

When I arrived home, I looked closely at the drawer and what was inside. I found what looked like a white salt powder and a vial, half filled with a thick, red liquid. The vial had a strong smell that reminded me of sulfur. The other chemicals were a complete mystery. There was a book that had nothing but dates and little notes next to some of them. The dates went back several years and ended about one year ago. The word "double" was written every month or so in the notes. I saw "TOTAL FAILURE!!!" written in large print near the beginning of the book. How could these chemicals and this book affect Jekyll's honor and sanity? I knew that Jekyll often ran experiments that did not work out. This seemed to be one of them. The more I thought about it, the more worried I became for Jekyll.

I sent my servant to bed and removed a gun from my desk drawer. I loaded it, wondering who this secret man would be who was coming to my home. I would take no chances.

At midnight, as the bells of London rang, there was a gentle knock at my door. I opened it and found a small man crouching against the pillar.

"Have you come from Dr. Jekyll?" I asked.

He made a sign that meant "yes." I asked him to come in, but he first looked over his shoulder at a policeman standing in the distance, staring our way. Then he quickly came in.

I was shocked right away by his strange manner and kept my hand close to my gun. In the light of the room, I saw him more clearly. I knew I had never seen him before. He was small, as I have said, and his face was hard to look at. He seemed deformed in some way. There was something very wrong with this man. My stomach felt weak as I looked at him. I felt hatred—no, I felt something stronger than hatred for this person.

This disgusting little man was dressed in expensive clothes, but they were much too large for him. His pants hung loose on his legs and were rolled up several times at the ankle. The waist of

his coat hung below his hands. The collar was spread across his shoulders. This creature standing in front of me was not normal. I found it hard to believe that he could walk around London without being arrested—just for the way he looked! His odd, twisted face was lit with excitement, however.

"Have you got it?" he cried. "Have you got it?" He grabbed my arm and shook it.

I backed away from him. The touch of his hand had made my blood grow ice cold. "Sir," I said, "I don't believe we've ever met. Please have a seat." I sat down in a chair, hoping that my horror of him did not show on my face. I tried to act normal and think of this man as a medical patient.

"I beg your pardon, Dr. Lanyon," he said more calmly. "I have been rude. Forgive me for acting so impatiently. I have been sent here, as you know, by Henry Jekyll. I believe there is a drawer…?" He reached for his throat and seemed about to panic.

I felt sorry for the man at that moment. And I was curious as to what this was all about.

"There it is," I said. I pointed to the drawer which lay on the floor behind my desk, still covered with the cloth.

He sprang to it, then stopped and put his hand upon his heart. I could hear his teeth grinding horribly. His face became pale and I feared for his life and sanity.

"Get a hold of yourself, sir!" I said.

He turned toward me and gave me a dreadful smile. Then he grabbed the cloth and tossed it aside. When he saw the contents of the drawer, he sobbed with relief. I was so scared, I felt as if I had turned to stone. He turned toward me and quietly asked, "May I have a measuring glass?"

I got up from my chair stiffly, and handed him a glass from the counter.

He thanked me with a smiling nod. Then he removed the chemicals from the drawer. I watched as he measured out some of the red liquid into the glass and added one of the powders. The mixture had a dull red color at first. As the powder dissolved, the mixture began to brighten and bubble. I could smell the awful fumes. Suddenly, the chemicals stopped fizzing, turned a dark purple, then faded slowly to a watery green. My visitor watched the process closely, with his eyes just inches from the glass. He smiled, set the glass on the desk, then turned and looked at me with an eerie twinkle in his eye.

"And now," he said, "to solve this mystery for you. Do you wish for me to stay and drink this? Would you rather that I leave? Is your curiosity too much for you? If you watch me drink, you will see things you never thought possible. This drink will save me from my nightmare, but I must tell you that what you will see would bother the Devil himself!"

"Sir," I said, trying to act cool, "your words and actions confuse me. I would be lying if I said I was

not frightened by your strange behavior. But I've come too far not to see this to the end. Drink from the glass and be done with it, sir!"

"Very well," replied my visitor. "Lanyon, remember the vows you took when you became a doctor. What you are about to witness is to remain our professional secret. As doctors, we've traveled separate paths. And now, you who have made *fun* of new ideas you could not understand—behold!"

He brought the glass to his lips and drank in one gulp. A cry came from his gasping open mouth. He staggered, holding the edge of the desk for balance. As I stared at him, he started to change—he seemed to swell—his face became suddenly black and it seemed to melt and move! The next moment, I sprang to my feet and leaped back against the wall! I raised my arms in front of my face to shield me from this sight! My entire body shook in terror!

"God help me!" I screamed. "Dear God! Dear God!!" For there before my eyes—pale and shaken, and reaching into the air with his hands, like a man brought back from death—there stood Henry Jekyll!

What Jekyll told me in the next hour I cannot bring myself to put on paper. I saw what I saw, I heard what I heard, and my soul was sickened. Yet I think about it now and I ask myself if I believe it. I have no answer. My life is shaken to its roots. I cannot sleep, and this most terrifying memory stays with me all day and night. I know that my days are numbered and that I must soon die. I'll die trying not to believe what I saw and heard. I will say this, Utterson—and I ask you to open your mind and believe what you read. Jekyll told me the name of the creature who crept into my house that night—who changed before my eyes into my friend. He is known as Edward Hyde, the fiend who is hunted for in every corner of the land as the murderer of Sir Danvers Carew.

—Hastie Lanyon

CHAPTER FIFTEEN

The Confession of Henry Jekyll

Utterson could not believe what he read. If what Dr. Lanyon wrote was true, then the dead man in Jekyll's office was not just Edward Hyde—but also Henry Jekyll himself.

With a shaking hand, he opened the confession of Jekyll and began to read:

MY CONFESSION

I was born in the year 1836. My parents were very wealthy and well respected in London. I was handsome, well educated, and hard working. My worst fault was that I liked excitement. I was

happiest when I was the life of the party, but I knew I could never be respected if I did not lead a serious life. I tried to hide my desires, and lived, instead, a double life.

I suppose that what I did in my earlier years was not so bad. There are some men who would even boast about such mischievous deeds. But I felt only shame. I kept my nighttime actions private, knowing I'd be judged harshly if anyone found out the truth.

I began to think deeply about these matters. I believed there was a fine line between the good and evil that existed in all men. I often thought about what I had learned in church growing up. Still, I was convinced that this must be a natural part of the human mind—to have two sides. For I was, in fact, living as two people. Both sides were very real. Both sides of me enjoyed life, whether I was healing sick people as a doctor during the day, or walking the streets of London looking for trouble at night.

My scientific studies led me to realize that man has two sides. I have a good side and a very evil side. I know that I am two people with two different reasons for living. I believe that

someone will discover someday that most people have not two, but even three or four different selves. These thoughts filled me with ideas. What if my two selves could be split apart? If I could figure out a way to divide into my two twin selves, I could live a happier life. When I wanted to be good, I'd be good. When I wanted to be sinful and reckless, I could do that, too. This way, I would always be pleased and happy with myself. This became my goal—to separate the two men and give each its own body.

I began to make progress as I worked every day at my laboratory table. I won't discuss exactly how and what I did scientifically, because the end result is incomplete. What worked for me might not work for someone else and might cause him to go completely insane. But I did indeed invent a powerful drug. I mixed several chemicals that I thought could change my body and mind into my other self. This was the drug that would free both parts of me—and finally bring me happiness, I thought.

Although I was sure the drug would work, I waited many months before trying it. I feared that I would get terribly sick or even die from an

overdose. And what if I lost my good side forever? I struggled with doubt, but the temptation was too strong. One day I bought a large quantity of a chemical salt which was the final ingredient for the mixture. Late one night I finally had the courage to test it. I carefully mixed the chemicals together, watched them boil and smoke in the glass, and drank the potion in one gulp.

I immediately felt pains in my body that I

cannot describe. My bones seemed to grind against one another and I felt sick to my stomach. I knew I was about to die! But then the pain and nausea were suddenly gone, and I felt better than I had ever felt in my life. I felt younger, lighter and happier in just seconds. I felt a freedom in my soul. I tingled from head to toe. I realized that I didn't have a care in my mind. My thoughts were wicked, but exciting. I stretched out my hands to feel this newness, and became aware that my sleeves were longer—no, I was much smaller!

There was no mirror in my room at that time. (The one that stands beside me, as I write, I brought in later so I could see exactly what happened during my change.) It was well past midnight, so I decided to venture from my laboratory office to my own bedroom in the main house. My servants were all sleeping so I knew no one would see me. I walked through the yard, into the house, and down the hallways, feeling like a stranger in my own home. I opened the door to my bedroom and walked toward the large mirror in the corner. There I saw for the first time the face of *Edward Hyde*.

The "evil" side of me, which I had become, was shorter and thinner than my "good" side, which was tall and well developed. My theory is that I had been good for most of my life, so my good side had lived longer, grown taller, and grown older than my bad side. Edward Hyde was simply smaller, lighter and younger than Henry Jekyll. Hyde had the deformed look of evil, but I felt no horror when I looked upon his ugly face. Instead I welcomed him. This, too, was a part of me! It seemed natural and human. In my eyes it was a livelier, more adventurous side of me. I became aware later that people found Hyde to be disgusting. This is because all men are a mix of good and evil. They recognized that Hyde was not a typical man, for he was pure evil.

I stood in front of the mirror a moment longer. I knew I had to find out if the potion would turn me back into Jekyll. Would it work, or was I to live the rest of my life as Hyde? I hurried back to my office. There I mixed another glass, drank it quickly and began to suffer the same pain and nausea. I looked at my hands and knew that I was once again Henry Jekyll.

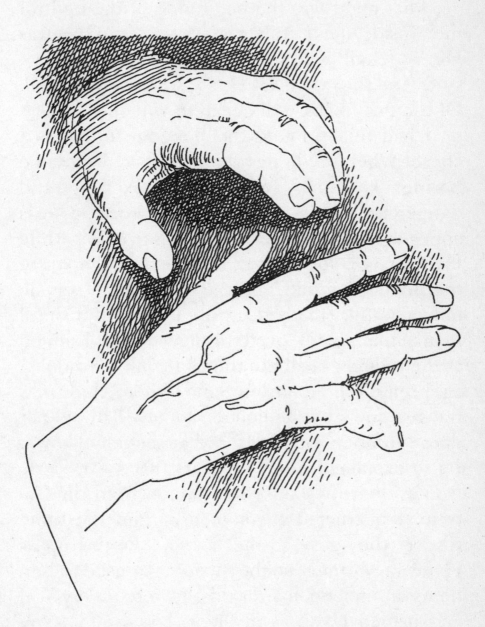

That night was the beginning of the end for me. Inside me I truly was two men. One was Henry Jekyll, who still had both a good and evil side. And the other was Hyde, who was only evil. Of the two forces, evil began to win out.

I had finally found the freedom to live as I chose. When my life as the good doctor became boring, I simply became the exciting and dangerous Hyde. Jekyll's life became less appealing to me. He was getting older while Hyde stayed young. But, all it took was a stir of the potion, a drink from the glass, and I was no longer a dull, elderly doctor but a youthful sinful man of the night. I loved this new power! I smiled at the thought of all the things I could now do!

I rented the rooms in Soho (where Hyde was tracked down by the police). I knew I would not draw attention to myself in that section of town. I also explained to my servants that a Mr. Hyde would be at my house in London from time to time. I instructed them to give him the same respect they gave to me. I even showed up as Hyde a few times, so they would get used to him being around. Soon after this, I wrote up my Will and named Hyde as my heir. I know that you

greatly disliked my Will, Utterson. But, you see, I had to make sure that if I could not turn back into Jekyll, I would "inherit" my own money and live on as Hyde. After I had taken care of these things, I felt completely safe to live my double life. I had found freedom.

Some men hire villains to do their dirty work. I could do whatever I pleased myself. All I needed was a second or two in my laboratory to mix and drink the formula. No matter what Hyde had done the night before, he would disappear and become the loveable and respected Jekyll once again.

The pleasures I enjoyed as Hyde, as I have said, were devilish. At times they were even against the law. When I would return from my outings as Hyde, I would often sit as Jekyll and wonder about what had just happened. This man whom I released and let loose into the night was nothing but a villain. He was purely selfish, pleasing only himself. His goal each night was simply to get drunk and cause pain to others. He was a monster! Henry Jekyll was scared sometimes by Hyde's actions. Still he knew that it was Hyde—and Hyde alone—who was guilty. Jekyll would wake up each day knowing what

had happened the night before. Sometimes he would try to correct the evil Hyde had done. So he slept with a good conscience most of the time.

There were warning signs that the double life I enjoyed was coming to an end. I felt a storm inside my soul but could not do anything about it. There was an accident one night that could have turned out worse than it did. I ran into a child on the streets and left her screaming in pain. A man witnessed my crime—the same man I recognized the other day as your cousin, Mr. Enfield. He stopped me before I could escape. A doctor and the child's family soon crowded around me. At that moment I was afraid for my life! In order to calm them down and save myself, Hyde brought them to the laboratory door and paid them with a check from Jekyll's bank account. To make sure this didn't happen again, I opened an account at another bank under the name of Hyde. By slanting my pen to the left, Hyde now had his own signature.

Two months before the murder of Sir Danvers, I had been out on one of my adventures as Hyde. I returned home very late, turned back into Jekyll, and went to my own room. I woke the

next day feeling very odd. I looked around my room, half asleep. I had the foggy idea that I was not in my house on the square. Something kept telling me that I was not where I was supposed to be. Was I dreaming? I felt as though I should have been in Soho where Hyde slept. But that

couldn't be... I smiled to myself and tried to wake up from this strange dream. I dozed off again for a while. When I finally decided to begin the day, the most frightful thing happened! I reached to remove my quilt—what I saw was a thin, dark hand with large knuckles and ugly veins, covered in hair. It was the hand of Edward Hyde!

I must have stared at it for half a minute in terror. Then I sprang from my bed to the mirror. What I saw made my blood turn to ice and my heart pound in my chest. I had gone to bed as Henry Jekyll and awakened as Edward Hyde! What had happened?! And more importantly, how could it be fixed?! I was shaking in horror. All the servants were up and my drugs were in my office in the laboratory! I could cover my face but could not disguise my size and baggy clothing.

Then, with a great sense of relief, I remembered that the servants were used to seeing Hyde come and go. I dressed as well as I could in my own clothes and walked through the house. The only servant I saw was Bradshaw. He nodded and gave me an odd look, for he had never seen Hyde in this part of the house.

Within ten minutes I was Jekyll once again and sitting down to breakfast.

I had no appetite. I couldn't get rid of this awful feeling of waking as Hyde. I began to realize the new danger of my double life. Edward Hyde was becoming more powerful! What if he eventually took over? Was that possible?

Things got worse after that. Once, early on, the drug didn't work at all. Since then, there were many times I had to double—even triple—the ingredients for the change to take place. At the beginning, the "changing over" took a little longer when I became Hyde. Now, it was just the opposite. I was slowly losing control of my better self—to my worse self.

I knew that I must make a choice between the two. My two selves had the same memory, but that was the only thing we had in common. Jekyll enjoyed the pleasures and adventures that Hyde gave him. But Hyde felt that Jekyll was boring and of no real use. Jekyll was the interested "Father" and Hyde the rebellious "Son." If I got rid of Jekyll, I would lose my friends and my dignity. I would have to throw away all of the finer things in life I had worked so

long and hard to achieve. To remove Hyde would mean giving up my secret pleasures.

The decision might seem easy, but there was something else to think about. Jekyll would certainly miss the pleasures he enjoyed through Hyde, but Hyde would not feel a loss at all if Jekyll were gone forever. The choice I had to make was like that of any person choosing between right and wrong. And like anyone with a conscience, I chose the better me. Yet, like most men, I did not have the strength to stick with my decision.

Yes, I chose the quiet, sad doctor and threw away the pleasures I knew as Hyde. But, deep down, I was not serious about my decision. For why else would I have kept the house in Soho? Why else would I have kept Hyde's clothes folded neatly in my office? For two months, I lived a moral life. But then I felt that nagging desire to be wicked. I missed the feeling of running into the dark night as Hyde. I could not deal with my frustrations any longer and finally, one night, I drank the vile liquid to release my other self.

Hyde had been caged for nearly two months. When I released this demon, I realized the mistake I had made right away. He ran from the room and into the night like a wounded animal.

Instantly the spirit of hell awoke in me and I went completely mad! I met a kind-looking older man and struck him with my cane. I struck him again and again. I felt a sudden thrill of terror as I looked at the bloody scene.

I left the dead man and ran to the house in Soho. I destroyed all of my papers and set out back to the house on the square, through the lamp-lit streets. Hyde was singing as he drank the potion. He again became the doctor. Jekyll fell to his knees with tears streaming from his eyes, feeling both grateful and sickened. He joined his hands together and raised them to God, asking for mercy and forgiveness.

I saw my life pass before my eyes at that moment. I followed it from the days of childhood, holding my father's hand, through the many years of my professional career as a respected doctor and citizen. I could not erase from my mind what had just happened! I cried and prayed, trying to get rid of the terrible images and sounds that were in my head. As I began to come to my senses, I suddenly rejoiced! Surely this would convince me, once and for all,

to be rid of Hyde. I locked the back door that Hyde had always used, and ground the key into the floor with my heel. I was rid of him for good!

The next day, as the news of the murder rang out in the streets, all of London became aware of Hyde. When found, he would be hung to die in the gallows. I actually felt relief knowing I would never allow that to happen. Jekyll was alive and well. Hyde would never be seen again.

I decided that, from then on, I would somehow make up for all the bad things I had done as Hyde. I looked for ways to help others. I entertained my friends once again. I gave my extra time and money to charity. Deep within me, I admit, I still felt the desire to act out some of my evil thoughts, but never again as *Edward Hyde*!

There comes an end to all things. I had tried to be good, but my dance with evil had already destroyed the balance of my soul. I was enjoying a fine day in Regents Park. It was January and the air was crisp and refreshing. The frost had melted and the birds were chirping. A quiet calm came over me, and all at once it was followed by a horrid sense of nausea. I began to tremble and shudder. When these feeling finally left,

I was very faint. I began to be aware of a change in my thoughts. I felt bold, and daring. I looked down and saw that my clothes were hanging loosely on my shrunken limbs. The hand that rested on my knee was dark and hairy. I was once more Edward Hyde—a known murderer who would be hung from the highest gallows.

I thought I would go completely mad, but Hyde somehow kept his wits. It was Hyde who understood the importance of the moment. Jekyll would have surely collapsed in terror. My drugs were at home in the drawer. How could I get to them? I rubbed my temples hoping for an answer. I had locked the door to the back entrance and had smashed my key. If I tried to enter the house through the main door, my own servants would send for the police. I knew I needed help and I thought of Lanyon. But how could I reach him? How would I persuade him? Even if I *could* make it through the streets without being captured, would he let me into his home? Then I remembered that I could still write in Jekyll's handwriting. I knew then what I must do.

I rolled up my clothing and held my large coat close to my body. I waved for a passing cab,

which took me to a small hotel on Portland Street. The driver looked at me curiously and I saw him bite his lower lip as if trying not to laugh. I snarled at him, and he ordered the horse onward. If he had not, I would have, without a doubt, pulled him from his perch on top of the carriage and beaten him senseless.

I entered the hotel and looked around. I met the eyes of the desk clerk and he looked terrified. He took my money, showed me to a private room, and brought me a pen and paper. Hyde was used to danger and evil, but had never been worried about being caught. He fought off the need to run back into the streets and forced himself to write two letters—one to Lanyon and the other to Poole. He took no chances and handed them to the desk clerk with instructions to send them by way of registered mail. He spent the rest of the day by the fire, biting his nails, waiting for midnight. He had dinner in his room alone with his fears. At last, when night fell, he set out in the dark corner of a closed cab, and was driven through the city.

Thinking the driver was becoming suspicious, he paid him and continued on foot.

He walked fast, dressed in his baggy clothes, through the back alleys, trembling and sick with fear. He counted the minutes to midnight. A woman called to him at one point, offering to sell him some matches. He spit in her face and she ran in terror.

Lanyon had gotten my drugs, and I became Jekyll again—in front of Lanyon. The horror I saw on my old friend's face did not bother me a great deal. I realized that my greatest fear was not the gallows; it was the horror of *being Hyde* that frightened me most. I made it home and slept through nightmares for many hours. I woke up in the morning feeling weak, yet refreshed. I still hated and feared the brute within me, and I had not forgotten the danger of the day before. But at least I was in my own house, close to my drugs. I breathed a sigh of relief.

I was walking across the courtyard after breakfast, enjoying the chill in the air, when I felt the change coming again!

By the time I reached my office, I had become Hyde. I drank a double dose to bring me back. And alas! six hours later, as I sat looking sadly in the fire, the pangs came again. From that

day forth, I would change with no notice, at all hours of the day. When I slept or dozed off, I woke up as Hyde. The change became less and less painful, and it now happened more quickly. The powers of Hyde became stronger as Jekyll became weaker. The hate between them was now equal. Hyde hated Jekyll as much as Jekyll hated Hyde. Hyde began playing cruel tricks. He destroyed a portrait of my father and scribbled awful notes in my favorite books. If not for the fear of his own death, he would have killed himself just to get rid of me. His love of his own life is wonderful. But I must admit, although he sickens me, I still feel his attachment to me. He knows I have the power to cut him off by killing myself. Deep in my heart, I pity him.

It is useless to write much more. The horror I am living is beyond description. And I think that the horror may have continued for many years to come—if not for one thing: My first and only supply of special salt powder began to run low. I sent out for a fresh supply and mixed the potion only to find that the color of the mixture I was so used to seeing had *changed*! I drank it anyway, but nothing happened. You will learn from Poole how

I have written to every drug store in London hoping to find the special salt, with no luck. I now know, without doubt, that my original supply was impure. It was that unknown compound in the salt that allowed my experiment to work, though I wish it never had.

About a week has passed, and I am now finishing this confession, having just used the last of the old powders. This is the last time, short of a miracle, that Henry Jekyll can think his own thoughts or see his own face. I cannot delay too long in bringing this letter to an end. There is always the possibility that Hyde will find it and destroy it! If this letter reaches you, it is with a great deal of luck. If I should change back to my evil twin while writing the end to this, Hyde may tear it to pieces. I'll finish it now and hide it, hoping that when Hyde comes back, he won't find it. Then again, perhaps Hyde will leave it be. Indeed, the doom that is closing in on both of us has already changed and crushed him. Half an hour from now, I know that I will become that hated man forever. I know how I will sit weeping and shuddering in my chair. I will pace up and down this small room which has become my coffin.

Will Hyde die swinging from the gallows? Or will he find the courage to release himself at the last moment and end his pitiful life using the poison I have left on the table for him. Only God knows. What happens next is in the hands of my other self, which I am so sorry I ever brought out of me. This is *my* true hour of death. As I lay down my pen and seal my confession, I bring the life of that unhappy Henry Jekyll to an end.

THE END

ROBERT LOUIS STEVENSON

Robert Louis Stevenson was born in Edinburgh, Scotland, in 1850, into a family of lighthouse engineers. Robert loved the sea, but not engineering. While studying law at the University of Edinburgh, he discovered another love—writing.

Stevenson's family was quite religious and strict, so when he grew his hair long and befriended writers and artists, his family became alarmed. Stevenson had also been sickly and frail since childhood, and his family worried about his health. Despite these concerns, Stevenson went on to achieve great success as a writer.

Stevenson traveled, in search of adventure and a climate that might ease his poor health. He married an American, Fanny Osbourne, who shared his love of travel, and supported his writing. Stevenson's works include *Treasure Island* (1883), *The Strange Case of Dr. Jekyll and Mr. Hyde* (1886), and *Kidnapped* (1886). The idea for the story about Jekyll and Hyde came from a terrible nightmare. He spent three days writing down this dark tale of good and evil.

Stevenson moved to the South Pacific island of Samoa to improve his health. However, in 1894, at the age of 44, he died there and was buried on a hillside overlooking the sea he loved.